CONSTRUCTION
MOVEMENT

Lee-Anne Spalding

FITZGERALD
BOOKS

Bethany, Missouri

Photo Credits:
Cover, Title Page © constructionphotographs.com; Pages 4, 5, 8, 14, 17, 19 © N/A; Pages 9, 11, 13, 15, 20, 21, 22 © constructionphotographs.com; Page 12 © Alistair Cotton

Cataloging-in-Publication Data

Spalding, Lee-Anne
    Construction movement / Lee-Anne Spalding. — 1st ed.
    p. cm. — (Construction zone science)

    Includes bibliographical references and index.
    Summary: Series offers text and photographs to introduce
science concepts as found at construction sites.
    ISBN-13: 978-1-4242-1380-1 (lib. bdg. : alk. paper)
    ISBN-10: 1-4242-1380-0 (lib. bdg. : alk. paper)
    ISBN-13: 978-1-4242-1470-9 (pbk. : alk. paper)
    ISBN-10: 1-4242-1470-X (pbk. : alk. paper)

    1. Hoisting machinery—Juvenile literature.
2. Materials handling—Juvenile literature. 3. Motion—
Juvenile literature. 4. Building sites—Juvenile literature.
[1. Hoisting machinery. 2. Materials handling. 3. Motion.
4. Building sites. 5. Machinery.] I. Spalding, Lee-Anne.
II. Title. III. Series.
    TJ1350.S63 2007
    621.8'6—dc22

First edition
© 2007 Fitzgerald Books
802 N. 41st Street, P.O. Box 505
Bethany, MO 64424, U.S.A.
Printed in China
Library of Congress Control Number: 2006940865

TABLE OF CONTENTS

CONSTRUCTION SITE MOVEMENT

There is a great deal of **movement** on a construction site. Workers and machines are always in motion.

Machines, like this **excavator**, can build or tear down.

SIMPLE MACHINE: RAMP

A **ramp** is a simple machine. Ramps help workers move tools and **materials**.

Ramp

RAMP MOVEMENT

Wheelbarrows are often used on a construction site. Wheelbarrows move up and down much easier on a ramp. A cement chute is a ramp, too. The wet cement slides down the **chute**.

Wheelbarrow

Ramp

9

SIMPLE MACHINE: PULLEY

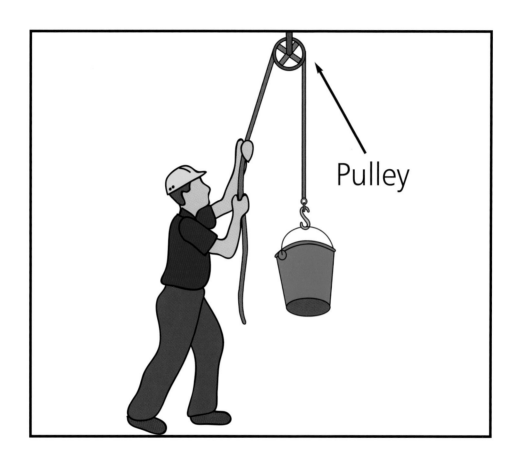

Pulley

A pulley is also a simple machine. Pulleys lift heavy materials. This pulley is hoisting a bucket.

This crane has a large pulley. Large pulleys **hoist** large things, like this piece of roof.

SIMPLE MACHINE: LEVER

Another type of simple machine is a **lever**. A shovel is a lever that workers use to move small scoops of dirt. Have you used a shovel?

Lever

The scoop of this bulldozer is also a lever. It moves large piles of dirt from one place to another on a construction site.

WHEEL MOVEMENT

Like the wheelbarrow, many machines move on wheels. This dump truck has six wheels!

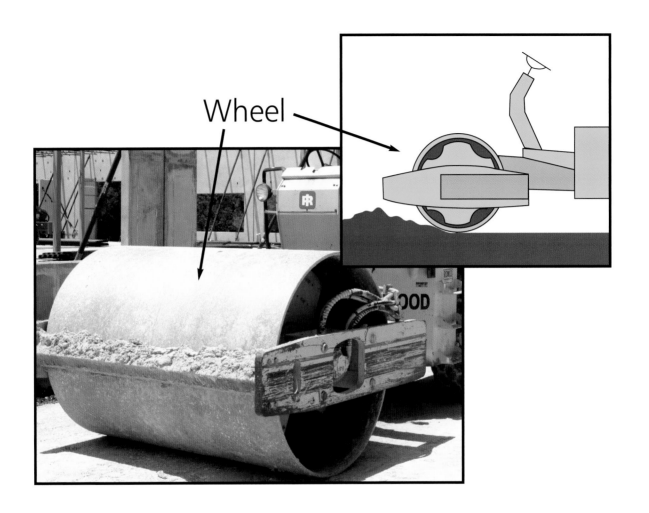

Wheel

A steamroller is an important machine at a construction site. Its big, wide wheel makes the dirt even and flat.

MOVING MACHINES

Some machines, like this tractor trailer, move other machines.

This dirt mover is moving to a new construction site.

WAYS MACHINES MOVE

Machines move in many ways. This jackhammer moves up and down very quickly.

Up/Down

The jackhammer's pointed end breaks up the concrete so that a new sidewalk can be made.

PEOPLE MOVEMENT

People are always in motion on a construction site. This scissor lift moves workers up and down to work on the building.

This cherry picker moves workers up and down, too. Like a crane, a cherry picker is also a lever.

SUMMARY

There is a lot of movement on a construction site. Machines and people move in many ways to get the job done. Next time you see a construction site, look closer to see construction movement!

GLOSSARY

chute (SHOOT) — an inclined plane or passage down through which things may pass

excavator (ek sku VATE or) — a machine used to dig out and remove

hoist (HOIST) — to raise or become raised into position

lever (LEV ur) — a bar used to pry or move something

materials (muh TIHR ee uhlz) — the elements or substance of which something is made or can be made

movement (MOOV muhnt) — the act or process of moving

ramp (RAMP) — a sloping way, plane or passage

wheelbarrow (WEEL ba roh) — a small cart that is used for carrying small loads

INDEX

FURTHER READING

Hudson, Cheryl W. *Construction Zone.* Candlewick Press, 2006.
Kilby, Don. *At a Construction Site.* Kids Can Press, 2006.

WEBSITES TO VISIT

Because Internet links change so often, Fitzgerald Books has developed an online list of websites related to the subject of this book. This site is updated regularly. Please use this link to access the list: www.fitzgeraldbookslinks.com/czs/cm

ABOUT THE AUTHOR

Lee-Anne Trimble Spalding is a former public school educator and is currently instructing preservice teachers at the University of Central Florida. She lives in Oviedo, Florida with her husband, Brett, and two sons, Graham and Gavin.